Elva: *[Confidentially.]* And I have a plan for getting out. For getting us both out.

Courtney: Yeah.

Elva: A wonderful plan. But I need your help. Let me find it. Here, in my dresser. Do you recall the Gray Sisters, from Greek mythology? They're in the story of Perseus. Three hags living in a lonely cave, with only one eye between them. When one wanted to see something, she had to borrow the eye from one of the others. That's the situation we find ourselves in here. My sight is leaving me. It's going quite quickly. Even large-print books are a blur. May is utterly incapable of reading. But you, dear girl—you have the eye. *[Pause.]*
Ah, here it is. Precious treasure. The book that will take us worlds away from North Dakota and winter and wheelchairs. A book that will strengthen your imagination marvelously. Take a look. The type is quite small, but your eyes are young.

Courtney: Bah-ed—

Elva: Like "bay." Baedeker. *Baedeker's Italy.* But you won't simply read it. No indeed. Let me explain. . . .

Mind's Eye

BY PAUL FLEISCHMAN

LAUREL-LEAF BOOKS

For Marty and Carol

Published by
Dell Laurel-Leaf
an imprint of
Random House Children's Books
a division of Random House, Inc.
1540 Broadway
New York, New York 10036

Visit us on the Web! www.randomhouse.com/teens

Educators and librarians, for a variety of teaching tools, visit us at www.randomhouse.com/teachers

ISBN: 0-440-22901-4

RL: 6.3

Reprinted by arrangement with Henry Holt and Company, LLC

Printed in the United States of America

March 2001

10 9 8 7 6 5 4 3 2 1

OPM

Mind's Eye

One

Elva: *[Languidly, to herself.]*
"So all night long the storm roared on:
The morning broke without a sun. . . ."
[Pause.]
A bona-fide blizzard, in the first week of
November. It's too early. Much too early. Even
for North Dakota. *[Louder.] Don't you agree?*
[Pause. She sighs. Voice returns to original
volume.]
"In tiny—" Tiny . . . First my eyes, now my
memory.
[Pause.]
In tiny something, something, something,
". . . all day the hoary meteor fell;
And, when the second morning shone,
We looked upon a world unknown,
On nothing we could call our own."
[Pause.]
Dear girl, are you awake? *It's nearly eleven.*

[Long pause and sigh.]
"Around the glistening wonder bent
The blue walls of the firmament,
No cloud above, no earth below,—
A universe of sky and snow. . . ."
[Pause.]
Courtney, are you awake? You are—I can see it.
At last! Dear girl. It's not healthy to sleep
so much.

Courtney: *[Voice flat and barely audible throughout.]* Where
am I?

Elva: Poor thing, don't you remember? You came
yesterday. In the afternoon. *Briarwood
Convalescent Home.* You've slept nearly the entire
time. . . . I'm Elva. Have you forgotten? . . . The
other bed is May's. She's out right now. She's the
one who touched your face and stroked your
hair. Remember? . . . She's got Alzheimer's.
Though I'd guess there are plenty of us here
who'd like to feel that smooth skin of yours.
We don't have any other patients so young.
You're a visitor from a far country for us.
How old are you?
[No response.]
I asked how old you are, Courtney.

Courtney: *[Long pause.]*
Sixteen.

Elva: I guessed seventeen. I taught high-school English
and drama for thirty-two years. I was just reciting
from "Snow-Bound," actually. Keeping myself
company. Look at the snow coming down out
the window. Can you believe it? I'm sure you
know the poem. . . . Don't you?
[No response.]
By John Greenleaf Whittier.
[Pause.]
It takes me straight back eighty years to Ithaca,
New York. When we lived in the big house out
on Frenchman Road.
[Pause.]
Did you grow up here in Bismarck?
[No response.]
Am I prying? Or simply talking too much?
Forgive me. I've been starved for talk, marooned
here with May. Holding a conversation with her
is quite a hopeless proposition. But I can enjoy
silence. Just watching the snow fall.
[Long pause. Then she starts up again softly.]
"The old familiar sights of ours
Took marvellous shapes; strange domes and
                towers

Rose up where sty or corn-crib stood,
Or garden-wall, or belt of wood. . . ."
[Pause.]
It's rather like being snowbound, living here,
you'll find. Trapped inside, the front door locked
so that the likes of May don't wander out.
Confined with a mixed lot of lodgers all taking
shelter from the storms of sickness and senility.
The flickering TV instead of the hearth. The
unchanging days. It's a winter without end. But
then, when I heard I'd be getting another
roommate!
[With gusto.]
"Next morn we wakened with the shout
Of merry voices high and clear;
And saw the teamsters drawing near
To break the drifted highways out. . . ."
The first thing I asked the nurse was, "Does she
read?" And when she said she was sure you did—
why, I felt I'd been rescued. I can't tell you how
glad I am that you're here.
[Pause.]
I didn't mean that I'm glad you've ended up
here. Of course not. Please forgive me.
[Pause.]
The nurse told me about your accident. I've
never trusted horses, myself. . . . I'm so sorry for
you, dear thing. . . . Then again, doctors can

work such wonders these days. A few weeks or
months of rehabilitation and you'll be winging
out of here like a bird from the nest.

Courtney: *[Long pause.]*
             Guess again.

Elva: You speak so softly I can't quite hear.

Courtney: *Guess again.*

Elva: Which means what?

Courtney: *[Long pause. Rote recitation.]* My spinal cord was
             severed completely at the first lumbar vertebra.
             [Pause.]
             I won't be flying. Or walking. Or leaving.

Elva: *[Pause.]*
             My dear girl. I'm sorry. I'm so very sorry.
             [Pause.]
             But what about your family? Surely you'll be
             returning to them.
             [No response.]
             What about your family?

Courtney: *[Long pause.]*
             I don't want to talk about it.

Elva: I'm sorry. Forgive me.
             [Long pause.]
             What a blessing, at least, that your injuries are
             strictly below the waist. That your brain was
             spared. The life of the mind is so much more
             sustaining than the life of the body. . . . A pretty
             girl like you may find that hard to believe. But
             you've actually been handed a golden opportunity.
             [Pause.]
             How I used to envy the pretty girls when I was
             young. The graceful ice-skaters. The beautiful
             dancers. I was quite plain myself. Crooked teeth.
             Disobedient hair. A disgrace and a public danger
             on the dance floor. I thought they had everything
             and that I had nothing. I burrowed into books
             while they frolicked. And how very glad I am
             that I did. Because now, when their bodies are
             failing them, they have no mental life to support
             them. I pity them. There are quite a few of
             them here.
             [Pause.]
             Do you like to read?
             [No response.]
             I asked whether you like to read.

Courtney: *[Pause.]*
             Not really.

Elva: What a shame. But you *can* read, surely. . . .
            Can't you?

Courtney: *[Pause.]*
            Yeah.

Elva: Then you can be a woman of independent
            means, like me, no matter what your body will
            or won't do. Think of Milton, blind but with all
            of English literature stored in his brain.

Courtney: *[Pause.]*
            Milton who?

Elva: Gracious sakes. *John* Milton. Milton was his *last*
            name. Perhaps the greatest name in English
            poetry. Prescott, too, was blind or nearly so.
            History of the Conquest of Mexico. I'm sure you've
            heard of it. Or think of Beethoven, deaf, hearing
            his glorious symphonies in his—

Courtney: Christ! What are you—my *teacher?*

Elva: *[Long pause.]*
            I'm sorry. Forgive me.
            [Pause.]
            I suppose I've never really retired from teaching.

[Pause.]
I only want to help you.
[Long pause.]
My point was simply that here you are, living in
this little room, stuck with two strangers not of
your choosing. But your mind can be as vast as
Russia and as crowded with characters as New
York City.
[Pause.]
Please don't go back to sleep.
[Pause.]
I don't mean to minimize what's happened to
you. Or to paint the future in glowing colors.
[Pause.]
It must be especially hard, given your good
looks. Your face, and your figure, and that lovely
auburn hair. I would guess that you're one of the
popular girls. And that you've had no shortage of
male admirers. Dances. Parties. Trysts and
intrigues. And then this.
[Pause.]
"And, when the second morning shone,
We looked upon a world unknown. . . ."
It must seem a strange world, indeed. But if
you're going to survive in it, you'll have to
remake yourself. You'll need to spend hours on
your mind, not your hair. It's there that you'll

run and dance and fly. You're going to have to
build inner resources.

[Pause.]

Perhaps you've heard of the poet William Blake.
"Five windows light the cavern'd Man. . . ." The
five senses, in other words. But you'll need a
sixth window, so that you can escape from your
cavern. You'll need imagination. You'll need it as
much as oxygen. Or more. We both do, actually.
I'm as unhappy here as you probably are. My
only good friend here died last month. I don't
like these dismal green walls or that sagging
window blind or the smell of urine or the aides
who manhandle us and then steal from us when
we sleep.

[Confidentially.] And I have a plan for getting
out. For getting us both out.

Courtney: Yeah?

Elva: A wonderful plan. But I need your help. Let me
find it. Here, in my dresser. Do you recall the
Gray Sisters, from Greek mythology? They're in
the story of Perseus. Three hags living in a lonely
cave, with only one eye between them. When
one wanted to see something, she had to borrow
the eye from one of the others. That's the

situation we find ourselves in here. My sight is leaving me. It's going quite quickly. Even large-print books are a blur. May is utterly incapable of reading. But you, dear girl—you have the eye.
[Pause.]
Ah, here it is. Precious treasure. The book that will take us worlds away from North Dakota and winter and wheelchairs. A book that will strengthen your imagination marvelously. Take a look. The type is quite small, but your eyes are young.

Courtney: Bah-ed—

Elva: Like "bay." Baedeker. *Baedeker's Italy.* But you won't simply read it. No indeed. Let me explain. When my sister and I—

Courtney: Not now.

Elva: I beg your pardon?

Courtney: I'm tired.
[Pause.]
Where's the remote?

Elva: For the television? My girl, that's for people who *have* no mind, who have to borrow one from the

networks. That would only weaken you.
Fortunately, you're in luck.

Courtney: What?

Elva: Dear Courtney—that TV hasn't worked for ages.

Elva:	This oatmeal really isn't too bad. At least you can't break a tooth on it. Which can't be said of some of the delicacies here. Just last week I broke another. On a soggy fishstick! Can you believe it? . . . Forgive me, Courtney, but headlines such as that are what pass for news around here.
May:	They make the sheets too tight tight tight!
Elva:	Another headline . . . It's true, it is rather hard to straighten one's toes. Sheila never leaves a centimeter of slack in the sheets. I believe she must have had a career wrapping packages before she became an aide. . . . That was Glenadine who brought the trays. You'll soon know them all. They become one's family, in a way. Glenadine is wonderfully consistent. Bad attitude, bad posture, and bad grammar. "Leave 'em lay there" is one of her staple phrases. Not to mention the double, triple, and quadruple negative. "By

rights she should be taken out and hung, for the
cold-blooded murder of the English tongue." As
Henry Higgins said. In *My Fair Lady* . . . That's
all you're going to eat?
[No response.]
Do you know the words to any musicals? Give us
a tune.
[No response.]
You probably have a lovely voice. Unlike the rest
of us. You should have been at the singalong
yesterday. If Stephen Foster had been called back
to earth to hear our "Old Kentucky Home," he'd
have fled back to his grave at a run.
[Pause.]
The poems you've memorized will serve you well
also. What do you know?
[No response.]
Some Robert Frost, surely. Some Shakespeare
sonnets? Perhaps a few ballads? They make fine
reciting. Do you know any Robert Service?
"There are strange things done in the midnight
        sun
    By the men who moil for gold;
The arctic trails have their secret tales
    That would make your blood run cold. . . ."

Courtney: *[Long pause.]*
        Don't know any.

Elva: *[Startled.]* Truly?
         [Pause.]
         It must be very lonely. . . . I can't imagine it
         myself. . . . It begins to snow and you hear
         "Snow-Bound" in your mind. You see a
         hummingbird and you hear "a resonance of
         emerald; a rush of cochineal." . . . It's as if
         poems are walking with you, arm in arm. There's
         no experience that hasn't been written of. They
         accompany you everywhere you'll ever go. Even
         through your surgery. Even into this very room.
         Even into death, and beyond.

May: Glenadine is the mean one.

Elva: I had scores of poems memorized at your age.
         Many of them quite long. I'm not bragging. We
         all did. Where did I read that Winston Churchill
         memorized twelve hundred lines of Macaulay as
         a schoolboy? My father could recite long passages
         of Homer in both the Greek and English.
         Mother favored the Brownings and Wordsworth,
         and the Walter Scott ballads. The poems of her
         youth.
         [Pause.]
         Truly? Not a single poem?
         [Pause.]
         Do you know the story of Scheherazade?

[No response.]
She was the Arabian woman who kept herself
from being murdered at dawn by a sultan by
starting a story late at night, a long, fascinating
story the ending of which she couldn't get to by
sunrise. The sultan simply had to know what
happened, so he let her live another day. That
night she finished the story, and then started
another just as good. And on and on, night after
night. Those are the stories of *The Arabian
Nights*. . . . You, my girl, must be your own
Scheherazade. You must keep yourself alive. But
how will you do so if you haven't any poems or
stories? . . . Or do you plan to simply sleep away
your remaining years? Or pass them with those
headphones of yours permanently in your ears?

Courtney: My Walkman's gone. Somebody stole it
last night.

Elva: No! . . . Actually, I'm not surprised. It's just the
sort of thing they take. That's a shame. . . . But,
frankly, Courtney, that machine was holding you
back. It was keeping you from tackling your
problems.

Courtney: It was *keeping me* from going insane.

Elva: And leaving you no time for reading and
             memorizing.
             [Pause.]
             My brother Terrence knew several whole scenes
             from Dickens, word for word.

Courtney: Goody for him.

Elva: He was always called upon on Christmas Eve to
             give us the last chapter of *A Christmas Carol.*
             [Pause.]
             And my sister, Rose. She used to entertain
             me with "The Pied Piper of Hamelin" time
             after time.
             [Pause.]
             That juice tastes odd, doesn't it? I don't believe
             it ever had any actual connection with an
             orange.
             [Pause.]
             Do you have any brothers or sisters?

Courtney: *[Pause.]*
             No.

Elva: That's a shame.
             [Pause. Gingerly.]
             Are your parents still living?

Courtney: *[Long pause. Sighs. Rote recitation.]*
             My father took off when I was two, for good.
             Then my mom married my stepfather. Then my
             mom died last year. Leaving me and my
             stepfather.

Elva: Dear Courtney. Poor child . . . At least you two
             have each other.

Courtney: Right. Try "stuck with each other."
             [Pause.]
             I never liked him and he never liked me. After
             my mom died, all we did was fight.

May: They say my dance dance dance lesson is
             tomorrow, not today.

Elva: More likely it was fifty years ago, May. . . .
             Has your accident stirred some paternal feelings
             in him?

Courtney: Are you kidding? No way he was going to wait
             on me and empty the pee from my bag. Or turn
             the house into a hospital with nurses in and out
             and him working at home. So he dumped me in
             here. His dream come true. And his pathetic
             girlfriend's, who couldn't stand me either. She
             moved in the minute I moved out.

Elva: Aren't there any other relatives who could take
            you in?

Courtney: Not really.

Elva: Surely you could demand to live in your home.

Courtney: *[Yelling.]* I don't *want* to live with those assholes!

Elva: *[Long pause. Gently.]*
            I see. Forgive me.
            [Long pause.]
            No poems or family for companions . . . Do you
            belong to a church?

Courtney: No.

Elva: What about friends?

Courtney: *[Long pause.]*
            They visited me in the hospital. The first few
            weeks . . . It kind of gave 'em the creeps. I don't
            blame 'em.
            [Pause.]
            I don't like 'em seeing me like this anyway. . . . I
            don't like anybody seeing me.

Elva: I would guess that your accident has had a

winnowing effect, separating the faithful from the faithless. That's a boon, actually. Especially where friends of the opposite sex are concerned. "In sickness and in health . . ." the marriage service says. Many couples aren't up to that promise when it comes due. . . . Do you perhaps have a boyfriend who's passed the test?

Courtney: *[Long pause.]*
We broke up. Before the accident.

Elva: I'm sorry.
[Pause.]
Do you miss him?

Courtney: Not really.
[Pause.]
I'm the one who called it off. . . . He was seeing someone else. . . . So was I, actually, sort of.

Elva: Well. I don't know quite what to say. Except that faithless friends are no friends at all.
[Pause.]
I'm not repelled by your condition. The talk of catheters and bedsores and all the rest. There isn't much I haven't seen in eighty-eight years. . . . When we have no families, we must

find support elsewhere. Sometimes in strangers.
We're all alone on this earth. We must take any
hand that's offered us. I offer you mine, dear girl.
I'll be your friend, if you wish. The faithful kind.

Courtney: *[Long pause. Flatly.]*
             Thanks.

Elva: *[Pause.]*
             I had very few friends myself when I was young.
             But I did have four brothers and Rose, my sister.
             We girls were the youngest. She was my constant
             companion. Very artistic. She was three years
             older and loved to organize neighborhood
             pageants and plays. She was writer, director,
             costume maker, set designer. She always made
             sure I got a good part. Dear Rose. She was an
             ideal older sister. Life was quite inconceivable
             without her. Now that she's gone, I find the
             memories of her coming up unexpectedly, like
             daffodils you'd forgotten you'd planted. . . . A
             marvelous memory garden to stroll through.
             [Pause.]
             Do you remember the book I gave you
             yesterday? It was Rose who invented the sort of
             journey I'm proposing that you and I take.
             During a blizzard, such as this, or when it was

simply too cold to go out, if we were tired of
reading our books, Rose would climb up on the
settee, from which she could just reach Father's
old travel guides. He was a classics professor and
he'd been all through Europe and the Holy Land
when he was a young man. She would pick out a
guidebook, decide on how much money we had
to start with—two thousand francs or pesetas or
what have you—and then she would lead us on
the most marvelous trips, following the
guidebook exactly: train connections, museum
hours, the cost of this or that restaurant. She
would figure out our route to our hotel on the
little fold-out map and tell us exactly what
famous buildings we were passing. She kept track
of all our expenses and subtracted them from our
starting amount. If we got dangerously low, she
would say she'd sold one of her watercolors to an
admirer for some extravagant sum. . . . And
that's what I thought you and I could do. It
really can be quite involving. Lord knows we
could both use the change.

Courtney: I don't know.

Elva: Just look at that snow. Still coming down. But
not where we're going. We could say that it's
spring in Italy.

Courtney: It doesn't really sound like my thing.

Elva: *[Pleading.]* I *know* it doesn't, but please say you'll
            try it. . . . I'm sorry to be badgering you. But I
            need you, Courtney. This trip is more than an
            amusement for me or an exercise for you. It's a
            promise I vowed to keep. Years ago.
            [Sighs. Pause.]
            Someone else will be with us on the trip, you
            see. Not someone here. Not at all. But someone
            who . . . who's died.

Courtney: Yeah?

Elva: Emmett. My late husband. That's his
            photograph on my table. That was taken at the
            Grand Canyon. And beside it is one of the
            drawings he made of me. Long ago. How I loved
            those jade earrings. . . . We'd always dreamed of
            going to Italy, but he died rather suddenly. He
            was only fifty-eight. He mentioned it near the
            end, never seeing Italy. He asked me if I would
            go for him. I said I would, naturally. But I
            simply couldn't bear to, not without him. . . .
            The years passed, and then I broke my hip. And
            then I got too frail to go at all. Once I came here,
            my only choice was to make the trip in
            imagination. This summer I had a little scare

with my heart and I realized I better not put it off. I must have phoned every book dealer in North Dakota before I found an old guide to Italy. The new ones are quite worthless. Too many pictures. Nothing left to the imagination. But when the book finally came, I couldn't make out a word with these eyes of mine. I began to fear I'd die before taking the trip. But then you arrived. My sharp-eyed savior.
[Pause.]
Emmett was quite charming, and quite knowledgeable about art. I believe you'll be glad he's along. If you'll be good enough to take part.

Courtney: *[Pause.]*
Nothing else to do.

Elva: Thank you, dear girl! . . . And naturally, if there's anyone you'd like to bring, please feel free.

Courtney: Can't think of anybody.

Elva: A friend. Or even, if you like, your mother.

May: My dance lesson is tomorrow, not today.

Courtney: My mother hated Italian food.

Elva: Though they say that the food over there is quite
             different from what we have here.

Courtney: [Pause.]
             Are you crazy? There's no real food. This
             is a game!

Elva: Yes, dear girl, of course. Rather like a cat playing
             with a little ball of tinfoil. Have you ever seen
             one—batting it about, arching its spine and
             backing away from it, pretending it's alive? The
             cat knows it isn't, but is entertained anyway. . . .
             Look here. They're late collecting the trays.
             Probably short on staff again. We have some
             time. Why don't we begin? Open the book to
             the chapter on Naples. That's in the south. I
             thought we'd start there, then work our way up
             through Rome and the north. Emmett
             particularly wanted to see Florence. . . . We'll
             imagine we've taken the steamer across the
             Atlantic and are just arriving in Naples. Have
             you found it? Paint us the picture.

Courtney: What do you mean?

Elva: Open the map—there's bound to be one—and
             bring us into the harbor. Tell us what islands

we're passing, on what side, and what's on them,
and where the lighthouse is, and whether we can
see Mount Vesuvius. That sort of thing.

Courtney: How should I know?

Elva: Use the book, my girl!

Courtney: I hate maps.

Elva: Then it's time you learned to love them. Maps
             are food for the imagination.

Courtney: And all the words on the map are in Italian.

Elva: Even better. You'll have a foothold on a second
             language before we're through.

Courtney: "Na-po-li." . . . What's that?

Elva: That, dear, means Naples.

Courtney: Oh.

Elva: That's a start. . . . But listen. Why don't you
             simply find the general description of the city
             and read that, somewhere near the beginning of
             the chapter. Until you get the hang of things.

Courtney: Physicians. Booksellers. Goods agents. English churches. Naples. *[All Courtney's quotations, in this and later scenes, are read slowly and with some difficulty. She slows even further when mercilessly mangling the Italian words; as the play progresses, her speed and comfort with the guidebook and with Italian increase.]* "Once the capital of the kingdom of Naples, now that of a province, the seat of an ancient university, of an archbishop, and of the tenth army-corps, with five hundred forty-seven thousand five hundred inhabitants, Naples is the most populous city in Italy. It extends for a length of two-and-a-half to three miles along the north side of the Bay of Naples, and rises in an amphitheatre on the slope of the surrounding hills. The site and the environs are among the most beautiful in the world. *Vedi Napoli—*" I don't know—

Elva: Keep going, don't give up!

Courtney: "*—e poi muori,* 'See Naples and then die,' is an old saying which the citizens are fond of quoting."
            [Pause.]
            That fits.

Elva: *[Pause.]*

In some ways, yes.

[Pause.]

But you, my girl, are learning to live and dream, not die.

[Long pause.]

Emmett and I stand at the rail. It's dawn, in the month of April. Still cool. The eastern sky holds just a hint of light. Only a few passengers are out on deck. Naples's harbor has just opened before us. Our sea journey is ending, the land journey finally about to begin. There's a sense of promise and excitement in the air. Emmett recites from Whitman's "Song of the Open Road." I lean back against him and can smell the sea on his tweed coat. My head rests in its familiar spot, just below his collarbone. When he speaks, I both hear and feel the words. " 'I inhale great draughts of space,' " he quotes. " 'The east and the west are mine, and the north and the south are mine.' " And then he kisses me, gently, on top of the head. . . . And he says, "And you are mine."

Three

Courtney: ... Chronological Survey of Italian History ...
Telegraph ... Post Office ... Mendicancy.
Whatever that is.

Elva: Begging.

Courtney: Guides ... Fees ... Intercourse with Italians.
You're kidding me.

Elva: My dear, that means social interaction. ... And
on that topic, I'll interrupt to say that your
interaction with Raymond today was really quite
shameful. If you don't mind me speaking
bluntly.
[Pause.]
He's quite charming. He's also quite well
educated. He reads the *New York Times* every
day and he subscribes to all sorts of magazines.
He keeps up on all the local issues. He often

writes letters to the Bismarck *Tribune*. Aside
from you, he's the youngest one here. Thirty-
nine, I think. A mere youngster . . . He was a
social worker of some sort. He had a car
accident, up north, past Minot. I believe that his
poor wife was killed. . . . He's genial, and
generous, and always cheery. Everyone adores
him. I would have asked him to read the
Baedeker book if it weren't for his difficulty
speaking. It does rather sound as if he's a
phonograph record played at too slow a speed.
But once you learn to understand him, you
realize that he has more to say than anyone
else here.

Courtney: *[Pause.]*
Forty-year-olds in wheelchairs don't turn me on.

Elva: My girl, he wasn't *trying* to "turn you on." He
came because he's outgoing and interested in
people. He'd heard you'd arrived and was quite
excited to have a young person to visit with for a
change. It was actually the third time he'd come,
but you're constantly sleeping. Finally, he came
calling when you were awake—and you scarcely
gave him the time of day.
[Pause.]
There *are* men who are looking for something

other than sex. . . . Have you never had a
friendship with a male?
[No response.]
I'll assume that's a "no." . . . I suppose that's not
surprising, at your age, with your looks. Trust
me, then. And believe me when I say that you
need friends like Raymond, who've kept their
minds fully alive in spite of their physical
problems. He's exactly what you should be
aiming at.
[Long pause.]
But *were* it the case that he had more than
friendship on his mind, I would think that most
women would find him quite attractive. . . .
And as for his wheelchair, it seems quite absurd
for you—

Courtney: You're right, it *is* absurd, but I *don't like* people
in wheelchairs, okay?

Elva: But Courtney dear—you depend on one
yourself.

Courtney: *[Pause.]*
Thanks for reminding me.
[Long pause.]
I thought we were going to Italy to forget
all that.

Elva: So we are. Onward. We were figuring out the
            money.

Courtney: *[Pause.]*
            Passports. Language. Money. "The lira contains
            one hundred centesimi."

Elva: *[Refining her pronunciation.]* Centesimi. Very
            well. Rose and I used to keep track of every cent.
            It was part of the fun. But I can't see any need
            for that now. After all, it's the last trip I'll take.
            Why pinch pennies? Why not stay at the
            grandest hotels? Very well. Let's get dressed.

Courtney: At nine-thirty at night?

Elva: *[Sighs.]* In *Italy*. Open your trunk and pick out
            your wardrobe.

Courtney: What trunk?

Elva: The one you packed back in the United States.
            You can put whatever you want in it. That's how
            Rose and I did it. . . . Would you like to know
            what's in mine?

Courtney: Thrill me.

Elva: Well, let me think. . . . Two linen-and-lace
           dresses, one white and one lavender. One fancy
           ball gown. Two broadcloth skirts. Navy-blue.
           Four white cotton blouses. One or two of taffeta.
           A black velveteen bolero like the one Mother
           wore. A hat trimmed with ostrich feathers, and
           something a little less flamboyant—a silk tam-o'-
           shanter. Petticoats, scarves, silk stockings. Batiste
           chemises and underclothes. A pair each of
           slippers and oxfords. Plus a pair of black evening
           pumps . . . I believe, however, I'll leave out the
           corsets. Ahistorical though that may be.

Courtney: And how are you going to lug a *trunk* down the
           sidewalk?

Elva: Shhhhhh. You'll wake May. . . . I won't have to
           lug it. Turn to the front of the book and see
           what year it was published.

Courtney: *[Pause.]*
           1910.

Elva: Well, then—that's the year we're traveling. And
           in 1910, there were porters and servants to carry
           your trunk. And draw your bath, and iron your
           blouses, and braid your hair.

Courtney: But I wasn't even born yet. How old am I on the trip?

Elva: Rose and I usually kept our current ages. But for this trip, actually, I'm going to change mine. I've decided I'll be twenty-three. That's the year Emmett and I were married. "Backward, turn backward, O Time, in your flight" . . . You can do the same. Pick any age you wish.

Courtney: *[Pause.]*
            What about . . . What about my . . . condition?

Elva: *[Pause.]*
            Your legs?

Courtney: Yeah.

Elva: Well . . .
            [Pause.]
            How do you see yourself?

Courtney: *[Pause.]*
            I'm not sure.

Elva: *[Pause.]*
            Imagine that you're in bed in your hotel room.

It's morning. A sliver of sun is bouncing off the washbowl across the room. You hear hooves and carriages and vendors below. You want to lift the iron latch and throw open the shutters and look outside. . . . Do you toss back the covers and walk to the window?
[Long pause. No response.]
Or do you sidle into the wheelchair beside your bed?
[No response.]
Or do you get there in some other fashion?
[No response.]
Are you sixteen? . . . Or are you younger? . . . Or perhaps older?

Courtney: *[Long pause.]*
I guess I'm sixteen.
[Pause.]
But no way I'm going to be in a wheelchair and have people staring at me all over Italy and crossing themselves when they see me coming. So forget the wheelchair by my bed. . . . I walk to the window. Just like anybody.

Elva: Very well . . . I didn't get my nap today. I'm tired, but I'd like to get going on the trip. Let's save time and say that we've already dressed and

taken breakfast. Emmett and I knock on your
door, we all descend to the lobby, and then walk
out into the sunshine.
[Long pause.]
Well, take us somewhere.

Courtney: Like where?

Elva: *[Sighs.]* Find us on the *map*. Walk us down the
street. Take us to a park. Or a museum. Tell us
what we're passing.

Courtney: Jesus—not the map again.
[Pause.]
The type is ridiculously small. It's like some
weird vision test. . . . C-7. Okay. I found us.
Finally.

Elva: Take us for a stroll along the bay. If it's not
too far.

Courtney: The bay? . . . For that we'd have to cross this big
street—

Elva: What's its name? Make the trip *real*.

Courtney: Riviera di Chiaia.

Elva: Very well. Present tense. *We cross the busy Riviera di Chiaia, weaving among the horses and carts and buggies—*

Courtney: What about cars?

Elva: Dear girl, it's 1910. Cars were still a rarity—certainly so, I should think, in Naples. . . . But perhaps the talk of horses makes you uncomfortable.

Courtney: They're not exactly part of my dream vacation.

Elva: Then we'll omit them as much as possible. *We cross the street—*

Courtney: And then we have to walk through the Villa Nazionale.

Elva: And what's that?

Courtney: Beats me.

Elva: *Then find the description.*

Courtney: All right, all right . . . There's lots of pages about Naples.

Elva: Which is no excuse for treating them roughly
             when you turn them.

Courtney: *[Pause.]*
             "Villa Nazionale. This public garden, laid out in
             1780, is a favorite afternoon and evening
             promenade. In the center is the Caffè di Napoli
             where a band plays on Sunday, Tuesday, and
             Thursday, two to four; summer, nine to eleven
             p.m. Chair: ten centesimi."

Elva: That sounds delightful. Shall we say it's Sunday?
             That way we can return and listen to the band
             this evening. So. It's April. We pass slowly
             among the flower beds, as if in a trance,
             breathing in the aromas, inhaling spring itself.
             [Inhales deeply.] I feel the sun on my shoulders,
             like a pair of warming hands. The bees are busy
             around us. Emmett sees that one's bothering you
             and waves it away with his hat. All men wore
             hats back then. Then he stoops to study a flower
             he's never seen. He's quite tall and thin. You can
             see that from the photo. But he wouldn't have
             had a mustache or beard at this age. His young
             face would have been shaved smooth with his old
             straight razor in the hotel that morning. . . . He
             takes out a small book from his coat pocket and
             makes a pencil sketch of the flower. He was quite

skilled at drawing. He's ravenous to finally set eyes on Greek and Roman sculpture. . . . Where is the bay?

Courtney: Right in front of us.

Elva: Really. Take us for a stroll along it.

Courtney: *[Pause.]*
            Well . . . I guess we'd go down Via Caracciolo. Then that becomes Via Partenope. It curves around. Then it becomes some other street.

Elva: Fascinating . . . Tell me what the water looks like.

Courtney: How should I know? . . . It's blue, okay?

Elva: Navy-blue? Prussian-blue? Robin's-egg? Turquoise? Is it flat or rough?

Courtney: *You* decide. I'm just guiding us.

Elva: Then guide us. What do we pass along the bay?

Courtney: We come to this wharf or something. . . . "The lighthouse at the end may be ascended by a marble staircase of one hundred and forty-two

steps, and offers a fine survey of the city.
Fee: 1 lira."

Elva: Up we go. Emmett counts the steps in Italian to
            practice his numbers. *Uno, due, tre, quattro.* We
            both studied Italian for a time. . . . At the top,
            we gaze at the city spread out before us. Emmett
            sketches it. He recites,
            "This City now doth, like a garment, wear
            the beauty of the morning; silent, bare—"
            And we laugh.

Courtney: Why?

Elva: That's Wordsworth, describing London. It's
            quite famous. But fitting here as well. The city is
            ravishing, golden in the sunlight. *[Yawns.]* At
            last, we go down.

Courtney: "From morning to night the streets resound with
            the rattle of vehicles and the cries of vendors.
            Strangers are often besieged by hawkers and not
            infrequently fall victim to pickpockets. The most
            motley throng is seen in the Via Roma, especially
            after dark. Late in the evening appear the
            lanterns of those who hunt for cigar ends and
            other prizes."

Elva: Of course, close up, the city appears rather
            different. Southern Italy is far poorer than the
            north. There must be swarms of beggars about.
            The mendicants you mentioned earlier. Mothers
            holding out a hand while suckling their infants.
            The blind. The deformed. Those who—

Courtney: Guess I'd feel right at home.

Elva: Now Courtney—

Courtney: "Most of the beggars are stationed at church
            doors. The importunate should be rebuffed with
            'Niente,' spoken firmly." What's that mean?

Elva: I believe that's the word for "nothing." But
            enough of this. Take us to a museum. It seems to
            me there's quite a large one in Naples.

Courtney: *[Pause.]*
            There's the Museo Nazionale. . . .

Elva: That's probably the one.

Courtney: *[Pause.]*
            But it looks like it's pretty far from where
            we are.

Elva: Then look up the streetcar routes. That's what
           Rose always did.

Courtney: Streetcars?

Elva: *[Sighs.]* Before your time. They were like buses.
           They rode on tracks and used electricity. I'm sure
           they had lines going all over Naples.

Courtney: *[Wearily.]* Hold on.
           [Pause.]
           Tramways?

Elva: That's it.

Courtney: Forget it! I'm not reading all that. There's
           a million different routes. I'm going to
           sleep.

Elva: Don't do that! We won't take a streetcar. We'll
           walk. Emmett would so like to see the sculptures.
           We'll say we just walked there.

Courtney: *[Sighs. Pause.]*
           Now I gotta go back to *that* page.
           [Pause.]
           "Admission, one lira." Wait. It's Sunday. Free
           admission.

Elva: *[Pleased.]* That's nice.

Courtney: "The ticket office is on the right. Adjoining is the cloak room for walking sticks and umbrellas. Ten centesimi. You then pass into a large vestibule, at the end of which are the stairs to the upper floors."

Elva: It's just as if you're there, isn't it? The Baedeker books are famous for their details.

Courtney: Like ten pages on just this museum. And maps showing all the different rooms.

Elva: Marvelous, isn't it? But I'm getting quite sleepy. Take us through a room or two and then we'll continue on tomorrow.

Courtney: "The first door on the right leads to the collection of marble sculptures, which occupies the whole of the right wing. Entering the portico, we encounter works of the archaic period. Number 6416, *Wounded Gladiator*. Number 6006, *Orestes*—"

Elva: *[Correcting pronunciation.]* Orestes.

Courtney: "—and *Electra*."

Elva: Famous figures from the Greek myths.
             Agamemnon's children . . . Emmett is entranced.
             He studies them from every angle, then takes out
             his sketchbook and begins to draw.

Courtney: "In front of the large, ornate window, note the
             Head of Medusa."

Elva: I doubt one could miss it. That hideous head,
             with snakes for hair and the glance that killed.
             Do you suppose the belief in the Evil Eye goes
             back to Medusa?

Courtney: The what?

Elva: The idea that a look from certain people can do
             harm. It was quite common, especially in the
             Mediterranean countries. Certainly in Italy.

Courtney: *[Pause. Interested.]*
             Yeah?

Elva: Let's leave ourselves there. . . . I really must go to
             sleep.
             [Pause.]
             Lights out . . . *Buona notte*—good night.

Courtney: *[Very long pause. Whispers throughout.]*

I walk up to the head of Medusa.
[Pause.]
I stand right in front of it. . . . And I look right
into her eyes.
[Pause.]
But I don't die. . . . It doesn't even hurt. . . .
[Even softer.] Because I'm as ugly as she is.
[Pause.]
I feel her glance go into me. . . . And then I
know . . . I have it inside me.
[Pause.]
I have the Evil Eye.
[Long pause.]
I wonder if it's true. . . . I walk up to the window
behind the statue. . . . I look outside. . . . A
carriage is stopped in the street.
[Pause.]
The carriage is pulled by a black horse. . . . He
turns his head toward the street. Then toward
me . . . I stare into his eyes, just for a second. . . .
He rears up on his hind legs and whinnies in
pain. . . . It's loud. People in the museum turn
their heads.
[Pause.]
I calmly walk away from the window and
continue strolling through the room with Elva.

Four

Denise: You should have been there, Courtney. We went
            over to Kyle's, 'cause his parents were gone, and
            everybody got totally smashed, and then, when
            we were going to leave, Lorraine couldn't find
            her keys, and we're all drunk and wandering
            around looking for 'em in all kinds of weird
            places and laughing our heads off, and Ronnie
            lifts up my skirt and says we haven't tried
            looking there yet, and I was so wasted it seemed
            like the funniest thing I'd ever heard. So we
            finally find the keys. They're like in the fishbowl.
            Don't even ask. Ronnie gets 'em out, but then
            somebody says the car will blow up if we start it
            with wet keys, so we put 'em in the microwave to
            dry 'em and all these sparks start shooting
            around and I'm laughing so hard I'm practically
            peeing and then Ronnie starts kissing me, and
            Brad had already left by then, so I kind of kissed
            him back, and it was really really nice. . . . And
            then, on the way home, we're going down

Washington and Christy threw up, right in the car, right on Lorraine's binder. Are you listening?

Courtney: *[Wearily.]* Yeah.

Denise: So she had to like dry out her homework in the oven to try to get rid of that vomit smell. Anyway, her and Jason are still together. Christy and Ben broke up, but that's old. Brad and me are going to the dance this Friday but I don't know what I'm going to wear yet. I kind of hope Ronnie doesn't go. . . . What *is* that thing?

Courtney: A standing frame.

Denise: Weird . . . How long do you have to be in it?

Courtney: *[Pause.]*
Ten more minutes.

Denise: What's it for?

Courtney: To get me off my butt for a change and put my weight on my legs.

Denise: Yeah?

Courtney: Or else my bones will get weak and start
           breaking all over.

Denise: Wow . . . They like strap you into it?

Courtney: Yeah.

Denise: You look like Mrs. Moskowitz at her podium in
           English.

Courtney: Thanks.

Denise: *[Pause.]*
           So—are you like done with school forever?

Courtney: I wish. . . . I'm in this independent-study
           program. I'll have the same old textbooks and
           homework. Some woman will come once a week
           and go over stuff.

Denise: But there's that freshman boy. He's in a
           wheelchair. He's got a locker and goes to classes
           and everything.

Courtney: Good for him. I'm not in the mood. I'd rather
           do the independent thing. But I'm sixteen. I
           might just drop out.

Denise: Wow. Cool . . . Maybe I'll join you.
            [Pause.]
            Weird mirror you got there.

Courtney: Yeah.

Denise: Why's the handle so long?

Courtney: Don't ask.

Denise: C'mon.

Courtney: *[Pause.]*
            Mirror, mirror, on the wall, who's the grossest of
            them all?
            [Pause.]
            It's for checking for bedsores. My back and my
            butt and the back of my legs and my heels . . .
            My PT gave me a pamphlet all about it if you
            really want to see some gross pictures of what
            happens to skin when you lie in one spot.

Denise: That's okay.
            [Pause.]
            What's a PT?

Courtney: A physical therapist . . . a career I definitely don't
            recommend.

Denise: *[Pause.]*
             So where are your roommates?

Courtney: Who knows where May is. She wanders a lot.
             Elva's doing crafts in the dining room. Making
             pictures out of macaroni. Gluing yarn. Stuff we
             did in kindergarten.

Denise: F. O.

Courtney: What?

Denise: F. O. Fun overdose.

Courtney: *[Pause.]*
             Never heard that one.

Denise: Really? . . . I guess it started after you left.
             [Pause.]
             So why wouldn't they move you to a room with
             a TV that works?

Courtney: This was the only empty bed.

Denise: Couldn't you switch?

Courtney: *[Pause.]*
             Nobody wanted to move into a room with an

Alzheimer's loony. Which I can now understand. She says crazy stuff all day. She puts on my clothes. I wake up and she's right there, staring into my face. Sometimes she thinks I'm her sister.

Denise: Weird.

Courtney: Once she threw her oatmeal across the room and all over my legs. Not that I could really feel it. You could put out a cigarette on my skin down there and I wouldn't know.

Denise: Jesus, Courtney. Don't talk that way.

Courtney: *[Pause.]*
            Just tellin' it like it is . . . And if you stick around a few more minutes, you can *see* how it is, when the PT unstraps me. . . . It's kind of like when they blow up some big building, and the whole thing collapses in a second. And suddenly there's just this pile of rubble.

Denise: Stop it!

Courtney: And then she'll rub in some lotions and maybe massage me, to hold back the bedsores. Maybe she'll replace my catheter and my leg-bag. That's

always a major thrill. . . . And if you wait long
enough, and you're really lucky, you might get to
hear us talk about my bowel regimen. It's really
pretty interesting. "How's that new laxative
working?" "Pretty good." "Let's talk about your
morning suppositories." "Let's. It's been ages
since we had a good chat about that." Fluid
intake. Constipation. And my favorite topic—
digital stimulation. That's right. Digital, as in
"using the fingers." I know it sounds gross, but
you have to do something to get those muscles—
[Long pause.]
Guess she decided not to wait.

Five

Elva: *[Gravely.]* "I will come on thee as a thief."
             [Pause.]
             "I will come on thee as a thief, and thou shalt
             not know what hour I will come upon thee."

Courtney: *[Pause.]*
             What are you talking about?

Elva: Death, dear girl. From the Bible. Revelation.
             [Pause.]
             Read on.

Courtney: "While the soft parts had decayed, their forms
             remained imprinted on the hardened ashes,
             which have been ingeniously used as molds, the
             cavities being filled with plaster and displayed in
             Pompeii's small museum, showing their attitudes
             at the time of the catastrophe: a young girl with a
             ring on her finger; an elderly and a young
             woman; a man lying on his face; a dog; a man

with well-preserved features lying on his
left side."

Elva: *[Pause.]*
They had names. And nicknames, probably.
Histories. Hopes. All unknowable. Nothing left
but their white plaster shapes . . . And yet, one
thousand nine hundred years later, we look at
them, and our hearts instantly feel their fear.
They realized they were about to die.
[Pause.]
Isn't that the essence of literature? Of all the arts,
really. Our ability to identify with characters, no
matter that they're separated from us by
thousands of miles and hundreds of lifetimes.
We may have no Mount Vesuvius looming over
us. It may not be lava and ashes we fear. But we
look at these forms, and we know what they felt.
[Pause.]
"And thou shalt not know what hour I will come
upon thee."
[Pause.]
People don't talk about it much. But that's
what's on many minds around here. When will I
die? And how? Will it be sudden, as at Pompeii?
Or drawn out and painful. Like the death of the
Roman Empire . . . We lie here like those white

plaster figures, under our white sheets, waiting
and wondering.
[Pause.]
Emmett was spared that sort of suspense. I
suppose he was lucky, on that count. He died of
pneumonia, of all things. Utterly unexpected and
swift. A Pompeii-style end.
[Pause. Rousing herself.]
But at age twenty-five, healthy and happy, on a
gorgeous day in May in Italy, his mind would
have been—

Courtney: I thought it was April.

Elva: We spent ten days in Naples. It's now May.

May: It's May May May. That's my month. How long
            will we be in Italy?

Elva: As I was saying, Emmett wouldn't have been of a
            mind to brood on the plaster figures all
            afternoon. We were young and in love. Our gaze
            was fixed on the present. He had a delicious
            sense of humor. I can see him, in that tomblike
            museum, speaking those lines of Andrew
            Marvell's. *[Imitating a man's lugubrious voice.]*
            "The grave's a fine and private place, but none, I

think, do there embrace." And then suddenly
clutching me in the most dramatic of embraces,
while the other sightseers gaped.
[Laughs. Pause.]
What else is there to see?

Courtney: *[Pause. Wearily.]* I don't know. The Basilica . . .
The Temple of Apollo . . . The Forum . . .
I'm tired.

Elva: " 'Tis the voice of the sluggard; I heard him
            complain,
'You have waked me too soon: I must slumber
            again.' "

Courtney: That's me.

Elva: Are you taking pain medication? Is that why
you're always sleepy?

Courtney: No . . . But that sure was good while it lasted.

May: Glenadine says Thanksgiving is next next
next week.

Elva: There's a point at which too much sleep is
unhealthy. I'm worried about you, Courtney.

Courtney: *[Sighs.]* Don't bother.
             [Pause.]
             "At the northeast corner of the Forum is the
             Macellum, a provision market." What's that?

Elva: Provision. Food. A grocery store. Let's go in.

May: Where's the food? When is lunch?

Elva: We just *ate* lunch, May.

Courtney: "Enter through the door at Number Seven."

Elva: We step in. It's nice to get out of the sun. It's
             pleasantly cool inside.

Courtney: "The walls of the interior are decorated with
             frescoes. Above are painted various edibles. To
             the left of the entrance, note the figures of
             Odysseus and Penelope."

Elva: We stop and look. Do you know the *Odyssey*?

Courtney: The what?

Elva: *[Sighs.]* Apparently not. Penelope was Odysseus's
             wife. She was besieged by suitors while he was off

at the Trojan War. Through twenty years of
waiting, she remained true. . . . I imagine her
hair to be wavy and black. Ribbons and jewelry.
Her breasts exposed. Or perhaps I'm seeing those
frescoes from Crete in my mind. I always
thought Mediterranean women the most
beautiful—I suppose because I was short and
heavy and red-haired, everything they're not. . . .
And yet Emmett did love to draw me.
[Pause. To herself.]
"My mistress' eyes are nothing like the sun;
Coral is far more red than her lips' red. . . ."
[Pause.]
In a way it was simpler, being unattractive. I
didn't have suitors hounding me, as they did
Penelope. Or you. Anyone interested in me
could only have been interested in the person
within. . . . Emmett also fell short of the
standards of his sex. He was reasonably
handsome, but not at all the steady provider
males were supposed to be. He was never able to
settle on a career. Terrible with money. An artist
at heart. Which I suppose is what made him
irresistible to organized, practical me. . . . My
mother paled when we announced our
engagement. She foresaw a life of barely scraping
by. And she was right. We traveled the country
one year, with Emmett painting signs to pay for

our keep. That's how we first came to North
Dakota. We were both from the East. The
starkness of the landscape quite mesmerized us.
And then, when the Depression came, and there
were no jobs in the cities, we came back here.
We lived in a little crossroads, north of Devils
Lake, nearly to Canada. They needed a teacher
and I had a certificate. I taught the whole town.
Emmett took care of the schoolhouse. He nearly
blew away in the wind, putting on a new roof.
Those were dustbowl years. Miserable times,
most people say. But we had each other. And
we were in love. At night, I'd read out loud while
he painted or chipped at his sculptures. Those
were enchanted nights. And charmed years,
despite all the hardship. That's what love does.
And it keeps on doing it. A good, loving
childhood fills you up like a good breakfast. It
gives you strength and sustenance for the adult
years ahead. And a good marriage does the same,
for the years of living alone that come after. I go
back to those years every day. Like a child
passing through the kitchen for a snack.
Something sweet and savory.
[Pause.]
Here I'm prattling away. And forgetting the
time. It's two o'clock. Time for our singalong.
Up we go—but not too fast. I get swim-headed,

standing up suddenly. Did you see my new cane, with the four little feet? It's really quite marvelous. . . . Maybe you'd like to join us, Courtney. You could learn some songs.

Courtney: No thanks.

May: It's snowing again. It always snows snows snows in Italy.

Elva: Just think how many songs you'd know after a year.

Courtney: Stephen Foster's not really my thing.

Elva: We also do some more modern composers. Victor Herbert. Irving Berlin . . . But I won't force you. Very well. *A presto.* See you in a while.

Courtney: *[Sigh. Long pause.]*
            We decide to walk back to the hotel. . . . We're tired. . . . We finally get—

May: I'm still hungry.

Courtney: Then start developing your imagination. Sit down in the *ristorante* and have a snack. Order a bowl of imaginary pasta.

May: I don't want Glenadine to give me a bath. She's
            the mean mean mean one. She's in Italy, too.

Courtney: She's such a witch, I'm surprised they let her in
            the country.

May: When do we come home?

Courtney: Never . . . Remember the story Elva told this
            morning? About that Greek woman or goddess
            or whatever who went down into the
            underworld, and she ate the food of the dead,
            and that meant she couldn't leave? Did you eat
            the lasagna at lunch today?

May: Yes. I had had had a little.

Courtney: Then you're in Italy for good. But who's
            complaining? It's a hell of a lot better than being
            here. You have no idea how lucky you are. Man,
            if I could switch brains with you—

May: They make the sheets too tight tight tight.

Courtney: If you say that again I'm gonna scream! *Listen,
            May. We're changing hotels. To where they make
            the beds just how you like 'em. Got it?* Hold on.
            [Pause.]

Elva put us in the Grand Hotel Pompeii.
[Mocking.] "Well-appointed," it says here. Not if
the sheets are too tight . . . Let's try the Albergo
del Sole. *Albergo* means "hotel." Only one and a
half lira a night. "Unpretending, frequented by
scholars and artists." Should be interesting. We
pay the porter to deliver our trunks. We each get
our own room. The maid asks you how you want
your bed made and you tell her *you want the
damn sheets loose.* Then you tip her fifty centesimi
to make sure she remembers, *which she does.* The
bed is perfect! *Molto perfecto!* You lie down, you
shut up, and you fall instantly asleep!
[Long pause. Softly throughout.]
Jesus. She's actually closing her eyes.
*[Long pause. There are brief silences after most
sentences, while she invents.]*
I go into my new room and unpack. It's night. I
lie down, but I can't fall asleep. It's chilly. I get
up to close the window and I look down onto
this courtyard in the back. A man and a woman
are standing down there. They're holding each
other, tightly. Not kissing. Just holding each
other, swaying a little, almost like a dance. They
don't see me. I watch them. They're both tall
and thin. They turn, slowly, and I can finally see
the woman's face in the moonlight. She has
sloping eyes and long black hair. She's beautiful.

I watch them forever. After a long time they sit
down on a bench, holding all four hands
together. They're talking softly. I want to know
what they're saying, but I can't understand
Italian.
[Pause.]
I'm a little hungry. I go down to the dining
room and ask for—where's that page with the
list? *Salato misto,* cold meat. And a plate of *uve.*
Grapes. When I'm done eating, I go outside. I
decide to take a walk through the ruins. I go a
way we haven't gone before. Left on the Strada
Consolare. Out through the Porta Ercolanese.
And then down the Street of Tombs. I don't
need a lantern—the moon is full. It's quiet.
Nobody else is there. There's no sound. Not
even any crickets. It's like being on the moon. I
like it. . . . I come to the Villa of Diomedes. I go
up the flight of steps. I stroll through the big
garden for a long time. Then I go into the house.
I stand in all the different rooms. It's my house
now. My villa. I go down the stairs to the cellar.
"Eighteen bodies of women and children, who
had provided themselves with food and sought
refuge from the eruption, were found here. The
supposed proprietor was found near the garden
door with the key in his hand, and beside him a
slave with money and valuables." The bodies are

gone. The cellar is empty now. It's dark and still.
I like it there. I stand without moving. Then I lie
down on the stone floor. I cover up with my
shawl. I don't want to leave. I wonder if the
volcano is still active. I listen for lava, but I'm
not afraid. It's peaceful there. I wait and wait. I
fall asleep waiting.
[Pause.]
Then something wakes me up. Voices. A
man's. Then a woman's. It doesn't sound right
to hear them here. I get up and tiptoe outside.
I see them, in the garden. The woman is
laughing, loud. I walk closer. She's completely
naked. She's posing. The man is sketching her
on a big drawing pad. It's the couple from the
hotel. They're artists. Her long back is white in
the moonlight. She's laughing so much she can't
hold still. He keeps chattering back at her. The
noise makes my ears ring. I feel furious. He
wants her to change her position. She turns. She
sees me. And my Evil Eye sees her. She holds her
position. The man praises her and draws. He
recites some long love poem in Italian. Finally he
finishes. He brings her her clothes. He puts his
hand on her beautiful shoulder. Then he
screams!
[Pause.]
Her body's as hard as . . . plaster.

Elva:	She isn't.
Courtney:	She *is*!
Elva:	Well, I think she's marvelous. And she's an occupational therapist. It's her job to be enthusiastic and positive.
Courtney:	I don't need to hear about some quadriplegic girl in the paper who's getting straight A's in college and is engaged to get married and can probably play the freaking violin with the bow in her mouth and is so incredibly cheerful all the time.
Elva:	But Courtney, dear, that girl is you. You just don't know it yet. You think that the way things are today is how they'll be for the rest of your life. But someday you'll change your mind about living here. You'll be ready to manage on your own. Living in your own apartment. Driving a

car with those hand controls she talked about.
Going to college. Shopping in your electric
wheelchair.

Courtney: When it's fifteen below and the wind's shredding
you and the sidewalk's not plowed? Like today?
Look out there!

Elva: *[Pause.]*
Is your family from North Dakota?

Courtney: Yeah.

Elva: Then summon up your forefathers' pioneer
toughness.

Courtney: My forefathers were secretaries and insurance
agents.

Elva: Think of Laura Ingalls Wilder in the *Little House*
books.

Courtney: *[Sighs.]* I don't sew. I don't cook. I used to hate
walking more than two blocks. I don't haul my
water up from some well—

Elva: I didn't say it was going to be easy. I'm speaking
of work, not miracles. But determination can

make the miraculous possible. Excelsior! Go
forward, like the boy in the poem, climbing the
Alps, braving all obstacles.

   " 'Try not the Pass!' the old man said;
     'Dark lowers the tempest overhead' "—
I believe that's right—
   " 'The roaring torrent . . .' "
My memory . . . But you know what I'm saying.
And you *have* made strides. Dressing, for
instance. And sliding along on that board to go
from your bed to the wheelchair. You've got
some muscle in your arms now. If only you'd
build up your mind the same way. You need to
furnish it, floor to ceiling. You need to be able to
live in it until you're back living in the world.
It'll keep you alive, like a respirator. And what a
richer life it will give you once you *are* out on
your own. But it's going to take effort on your
part. Which is why I was so disappointed when
your teacher came yesterday. I couldn't help but
overhear. And I couldn't help but agree with the
lecture she gave you. I so rarely see you at your
schoolwork. You, who have all the time in the
world! Precious time—and the eyes to make use
of it! You could be learning a language—or two,
or three. Or reading all of Shakespeare. Or all of
Allen Ginsberg, if you'd rather. Or making your
way through the Bach cantatas or writing a

journal or writing to Congress or teaching
yourself calculus or studying the Talmud . . .
You don't seem to have any *goals* for yourself.
You so blithely squander—

Courtney: *[Loudly.]* "—which leads us into the Piazza
Colonna, one of the liveliest squares in
Rome, named for the Column of Marcus
Aurelius—"

Elva: Courtney.

Courtney: "—which rises in its center, ninety-eight feet in
height, consisting of twenty-eight blocks,
embellished with scenes of the Emperor's wars
against the Germanic tribes of the Danube."

Elva: Dear girl—

Courtney: "Proceeding west to the Piazza di Monte Citorio,
we pass the Egyptian Obelisk, eighty-four feet
in height, then go southward, take the first turn
to the right, cross the small Piazza Capranica,
and, bearing left, reach the Piazza of the
Pantheon."

Elva: Where Emmett and I catch up with you. And
where we all rest. And collect ourselves.

[Long pause.]
Would you like to go in?

Courtney: *[Pause.]*
Go in what?

Elva: Into the Pantheon.

Courtney: Not if it's another museum. Even imaginary
museums bore me. And you can tell my teacher I
said so.

Elva: It's an ancient Roman temple, not a museum.
One of the most famous buildings in the world.
It's round. When I was young we had an
engraving of the interior on the wall, over the
mantelpiece. My father bought it when he was in
Rome. "The most beautiful building in the
world," he used to say. The Greeks and Romans
were in love with symmetry—and what could be
more symmetrical than a circle? Every point on a
circle is the same distance from the center. The
most perfect of shapes. Now, a circle in three
dimensions we call a . . . *[Waiting for answer.]*

Courtney: Don't ask me.

Elva: A sphere, dear girl. A sphere. And the dome of

the Pantheon is a perfect sphere—the upper half of a sphere, that is—set on top of a cylindrical wall. Cylinders come from the circle as well. And the *height* of that wall is such that, were the bottom half of the sphere to exist, its bottommost point would *just* touch the floor. I can still hear Father explaining it. Everything in perfect proportion. And all derived from the circle, do you see?

[No response.]

The Renaissance builders studied the Pantheon. They fell in love with symmetry, too. Everything perfectly proportioned and balanced. They adored the circle. You must have seen that famous drawing by Leonardo da Vinci of a man with his legs and arms stretched out, fitting perfectly inside a circle. They loved domes—three-dimensional circles. Michelangelo's dome on St. Peter's must be the most famous in the world. Where we went yesterday.

Courtney: "The Pantheon's interior, open until twelve and for two hours in the late afternoon, is lighted by a single aperture twenty-nine feet in diameter in the center of the dome, producing a sublime effect that has captivated viewers for two millennia."

Elva: Think of it. Father stood there, bathed in that
            light, perhaps with that very Baedeker in his
            hands. And now Emmett and I are there. And
            you as well.

Courtney: And somebody else. Look what just fell out of
            the book.

Elva: What is it?

Courtney: "Società Romana Tramways Omnibus. Ten C."
            Must be ten centesimi. It looks like a bus ticket.

Elva: Really!

Courtney: Number 010486. *"Conservare intatto il biglietto."*

Elva: Keep this ticket intact, I would guess. Advice
            that was certainly well taken.

Courtney: So let's see where this person went. Looks like
            line number fourteen. We walk out of the
            Pantheon and catch the streetcar. Gotta find the
            list of routes.
            [Pause.]
            "Line fourteen. From the Station, by the Piazza
            delle Terme, Via Nazionale—"

Elva: But what about the touring plan in the book?
            We were on the eighth day. That way we're sure
            to see all the important sites.

Courtney: "—the Quirinal Tunnel, Via Due Macelli, Piazza
            di Spagna, page 210." We get off there.

Elva: Emmett wouldn't have wanted to miss anything.
            He'd—

Courtney: He'd have been ready to break out of the
            routine. . . . We look around. We have no idea
            where we are. We start walking. The clouds are
            really dark. A few raindrops come down. I forgot
            to bring the parasol I bought back in Naples.
            Then it starts to pour. . . . Page 210 . . . We see a
            church up ahead. They're always open. We make
            a run for it—or more of a trot, with our long
            dresses. We go in out of the rain. It turns out
            we're in the Santissima Trinità dei Monti. We sit
            in the pews. People come in and kneel and pray.
            Some of them pay to light candles. We whisper,
            guessing what they're praying for.
            [Pause.]
            Slowly, we get dry. Then we hear a rumble.
            Then the church begins to shake.

Elva: Really.

Courtney: The chandeliers jingle. Bits of plaster fall from
            the roof. Then it stops. Everyone's looking at
            each other. The church has two towers. We
            decide to go up. It's fifteen flights of stairs.
            Halfway up, you and Emmett get tired and
            decide to go back. But I keep going. When I get
            to the top and step outside, I can see practically
            all of Rome. And suddenly I notice smoke, way
            off. And then it hits me. There's been an
            earthquake.

Elva: Courtney—stop.

Courtney: I look all around. And there, in the distance, is
            the Pantheon. And it looks like part of its wall
            has collapsed. And that its dome has cracked and
            fallen in on one side. And its perfect symmetry
            and perfect, beautiful proportions are ruined.

Elva: They aren't!

Courtney: Someone in the church must have prayed for it.
            And their prayer was answered.

Elva: It most certainly was not! Please close the book.
            That's *quite* enough sightseeing for today.

Courtney: I don't feel like quitting. I'm just getting

started. . . . You and Emmett stay in the church, but I go out. "To the southeast runs the Via Sistina, while before us are the famous Spanish Steps, with their flowers and picturesque parapets." I go down the steps. The storm is over. The sun's out again. I'm hungry. I come to a small café and go in. I order in Italian—*zuppa, arrosto di vitello, vino.* The waiter understands me. I read the Baedeker while I eat. . . . I'm tired of museums and churches. I flip to the section of things to do on the outskirts of Rome. I stop at the description of the Tivoli waterfalls. It sounds quite beautiful. I make up my mind and mark the place in the book. I decide that I'll take the steam tramway there. And that I'll go by myself.

Seven

Courtney: We're on the train to Florence. We've just passed through the town of Orte. . . . Actually, it looks like you have to change trains there. *[Imitating Elva's voice.]* "Find out, then. Make the trip real, dear girl."

[Pause.]

We changed trains in Orte. We're at mile fifty-two north of Rome. It's summer. It's late afternoon. There are four other people in our compartment. It's crowded in there and hot. The sun's coming in the windows. I decide to find a compartment on the shady side. "Very well," says Emmett. He smiles at me. Elva is asleep, leaning against him. *[Imitating Elva.]* "Am I? How delightful. I can still remember the smell of his tweed coat."

[Pause.]

I go out the door and walk down the corridor. The sound of the train is loud when you pass between cars. Two cars down I find a nearly

empty compartment. I go in. It's much cooler
there. I sit down. There's only one other person
in it. A man. About twenty years old. He's
eating. He has a little picnic basket beside him
on the seat. He reaches into the basket and hunts
around a long time for something. The whole
time, his eyes are on the floor. It's weird. His
hand is sort of like an elephant's trunk, searching
on its own. Then I see it, up on the rack with his
luggage. A white cane. He's blind.
[Pause.]
"Are you hungry?" he asks. He speaks in perfect
English.
"How did you know I'm not Italian?"
"Your perfume. And the rustle of your petticoat.
They use different fabric over here." It turns out
he's American, from Chicago. We introduce
ourselves. His name's Edward. I'm sitting across
from him. I'm starving. He hands me some
bread. His hand knows right where I am. He's
tall and thin, in a white suit. He has a little blond
beard. I try not to stare at him, even though I
could without him knowing. He gets out a little
knife and peels a pear. We talk. It turns out he's
going to Florence, too.
[Pause.]
We're in the countryside. It's beautiful. He asks
me to tell him what we're passing. At mile fifty-

eight and a half out of Rome we go through the
village of Nera Montero. We're following the
Nera River. Evergreen oaks on the hills. Then,
on the right, the remains of the Bridge of
Augustus. "At mile sixty-two we pass the village
of Narni, *Narnia* in Roman times, 785 feet,
perched on a rock high above the left bank of the
Nera." I describe everything we see. Farmers in
the fields. Horses grazing. Kids waving at the
train. He says he likes the sound of my voice.
[Pause.]
We come to the town of Terni. The train stops
for ten minutes. Edward says it's a shame we
won't get to see the famous waterfalls nearby.
While we're waiting, I use the Baedeker to lead
us on an imaginary trip there. I have us take the
electric tramway. "Getting off, we follow the cart
road, cross the Nera, then ascend steeply, and
finally come to the stone pavilion, with its
magnificent view of the falls and the whole Nera
valley." I make up what the falls are like. He says
he can almost feel the spray on his face. He's
smiling. The train leaves the station. But he says
not to tell him what we're passing. He'd rather
stay at the falls. So we stay. I say that we've
brought his picnic basket. It's tiny, but I have us
pull tons of food out of it. Roast chickens, a huge
sausage, a long loaf of bread, figs, bottles of wine.

He says I have an excellent imagination. He says
he's had to live in his mind, too, because of being
blind. He takes over for a while. He pulls this
huge circle of cheese out of the basket and invites
all the other tourists at the falls to have some. He
invents their names and why they're there and
makes up this long conversation we all have. He
has himself be blind, even though he doesn't
have to. He doesn't seem to mind. Neither do
the others. We all talk and eat and laugh. Then I
take over. Then him. Then me. It's great.
[Pause.]
The train keeps clacking away. It's dark outside
now, but I don't turn the compartment's light
on. Edward asks if I went to the waterfalls at
Tivoli. I tell him I did. We figure out that we
were there on the same day. Then he asks if I
went to any operas in Rome. I tell him how we
saw *La Bohème*. He says that's his favorite opera.
He starts telling the story, just like Elva. His
hands move a lot when he talks, like dancers.
When he tells about Rodolfo and Mimi falling in
love and him warming her cold hands, it looks
like he's holding his hands out toward me. It's
dark in the train compartment. I'm not sure if
it's just one of his gestures. . . . But I hold out
my hands. . . . And he takes them. And he
squeezes them. . . . And it's like our hands are

talking to each other. Back and forth. For a long
time. And he rubs mine, just like Rodolfo did.
[Pause.]
And I cross over to his bench. And I tell him he
doesn't even know what I look like. . . . And he
says, "What does that matter?"
[Pause.]
I remove my hatpin and take off my hat. And I
lean against him. And he puts his arms around
me. My whole body's smiling. And we stay that
way for hours. Just holding each other. I don't
need anything more. We listen to the train, and
talk now and then, softly, right into each other's
ears. . . . And I remember what Elva said, how
love wasn't over for me.

Eight

Courtney: Hey. What . . . What are you doing?

Duane: Well, look who woke up.

Courtney: Who are you?

Duane: Shhhh.

Courtney: What time is it?

Duane: Two-thirty.

Courtney: Do you work here?

Duane: Yeah.

Courtney: Doing what?

Duane: Night janitor.

Courtney: I never saw you before.

Duane: But I've seen you. I stand and look at you almost
            every break. And let me tell you. You're the *only*
            thing worth looking at in the whole place. Bunch
            of old dried-up Egyptian mummies.

Courtney: You don't say.

Duane: There's just you. You . . . and me. You can't
            really see me with the lights low like this. My
            hair's blond. Six feet, 158 pounds. I work out
            four days a week.

Courtney: Wow. A member of the master race. I'm
            impressed.

Duane: What?

Courtney: And what were you fiddling with on my table?

Duane: Just a little something I was leaving for
            you. A card.

Courtney: Look at that. And it's got a little poem on it. Let
            me hit my light. . . .
                "There's something in my heart
                that I'd really like to say.

It's difficult to start,
but here goes anyway. . . ."
Did you write that?

Duane: No, but I picked it out. You know.
There's more.

Courtney: Do you give one to everybody here? Like cards
from the garbageman?

Duane: Nope. Just you . . . The rest of the hags around
here about make me gag.

Courtney: Is that right?

Duane: Yep.

Courtney: Grind 'em up for fertilizer?

Duane: You got it.

Courtney: Hog feed?

Duane: *[Laughs.]* Don't know that hogs would
touch 'em.
[Laughs.] Say. You already got a boyfriend?

Courtney: Nope.

Duane: Well, any time you want to go for a gallop, just
            let me know. We'd have to be quick, but it don't
            usually take me—

Courtney: Pardon me if I'm making you gag, but I don't
            have any feeling below the waist.

Duane: *[Pause.]*
            I heard that from one of the nurses. . . . But then
            I got to thinking . . . that maybe it might be
            different than you think. You might . . . It might
            turn out you like it. Might be real nice for you.

Courtney: *[Disbelieving.]* For *me?*
            [Pause.]
            That is just *so sweet* of you to be thinking of *me*
            and *my* needs. *Awfully* sweet. And I sure will
            remember your *generous* offer.

Duane: Are you making—

Courtney: But I should tell you the truth. I'm one of the
            ugly ones. You'd know it if you saw my scars or
            saw me try to stand up. And I do have a
            boyfriend. His name's Edward. He had an
            accident, like me. He's blind. He's skinny and he
            never works out. He's one of the ones you'd feed
            to the hogs. We both are.

Duane: Is that a fact.
            [Pause.]
            Well then. Guess I've been wasting my time.

Courtney: Looks like it.

Duane: Then I guess I'll be going.

Courtney: Good idea.

Duane: You and Edward have yourselves a nice trip to
            the glue factory.

Courtney: And he knows more about love than you
            ever will.
            [Pause.]
            And he doesn't buy his poems from Hallmark!

Nine

Elva: Do you remember the story? Clever Perseus
           never looked at her, but only at her reflection on
           his shield. That's how he avoided Medusa's gaze.
           And so he safely approached—and lopped off her
           head with his sword. Isn't he standing on her
           crumpled body?

Courtney: *[Keyed up.]* It doesn't say. Can we move on?

Elva: I believe he is. It's a very famous statue. I'm sure
           you've seen pictures of it. He's holding his sword
           in one hand, and raising Medusa's snaky head
           high with the other—and showing off his
           magnificent naked physique for all of Florence to
           admire. It was the Renaissance artists, you know,
           who gave us back the human body. For a
           thousand years there'd been no life-sized nude
           sculptures. Imagine that. But Cellini and
           Donatello and Michelangelo gloried in the body

and celebrated its beauty, just as the Greeks and
Romans had.

Courtney: Great.

Elva: *[Pause.]*
Emmett makes a sketch of the statue. Then he
makes another from a different angle. We talk
about the Greeks' fertile imagination for
monsters. Harpies, Hydra, Cyclops, the—

Courtney: "Crossing the Via de Ninna, we come to the
entrance to the Uffizi Gallery—"

Elva: What *is* your hurry?

Courtney: You *said* we had to go there. So let's get it
over with.

Elva: That's hardly the proper attitude to take
toward—

Courtney: "We enter the second door to the left, under the
east arcade, from which we mount a staircase of
126 steps, or alternatively, take the lift for half a
lira. Both in extent and value, this is one of the
world's greatest collections. Raphael, da Vinci—"

Elva: Are you sure you wouldn't rather rest, or do
            something else? Bingo will be starting—

Courtney: "—Michelangelo, Titian, Botticelli—"
            [Pronounced "Bottiselli."]

Elva: "Botti*chel*li." But what's the rush? Let's take that
            long stairway, not the elevator, and linger over
            the fact that we're finally here. Florence was
            Mecca for Emmett. The Uffizi would have been
            its holiest temple. I can feel him vibrating with
            excitement. He'd—

Courtney: "From the highest landing we pass through two
            vestibules to the East Corridor. The first door to
            the left of the entrance leads to the two rooms of
            Venetian art. Number 575, Lorenzo Lotto, *Holy
            Family*. Number 630, Giorgione, *Judgment of
            Solomon*. Number 592, Sebastiano del Piombo,
            Death of Adonis. Number 626, Titian, *Flora*, a
            Venetian woman, half-undressed, with flowers in
            her hand. Number—"

Elva: Slow down, Courtney! We're not running a race.
            Let's stand in front of that last one a while. The
            woman holding the flowers. I'm not familiar
            with it, but I can almost see it. Titian made such

marvelous use of color. I picture her outdoors,
in a meadow. Rich greens around her, and the
sky brilliant blue . . . Did you know that
medieval painters often painted the sky gold?
It represented heaven for them, the home of
God, a realm completely removed from the
world of flesh and sin below. But the artists
of the Renaissance embraced this world. They
gave us back the blue skies we know. How
they would have loved the Dakota sky.
Especially—

Courtney: "Room Four. Tuscan art. Adjoining is the
Lorenzo Monaco room. Note especially the altar-
pieces by Fra Angelico. To the left we enter the
Botticelli *["Bottiselli" again]* room—"

Elva: Bo-ti-*chel*-li. *Chel.* Are you even listening?

Courtney: "—containing some of his finest work, first
and foremost *The Birth of Venus.* Note also
number 3436—"

Elva: Wait—go back. We *can't* dash past that one.
You've seen copies of it a thousand times, I'm
sure. Venus standing on that scallop shell, riding
over the ocean, with her head tilted and her hair
flowing . . . Do you know the painting?

Courtney: Actually, I think I do. And actually, I think I've
            seen enough beautiful naked Greeks for one day.

Elva: Well, Emmett and I are *quite* excited to see it.
            We stand before it. It's strange, setting eyes on a
            famous painting one has only known through
            reproductions. You can't quite believe you're
            actually there. The painting is quite large, I
            believe. There are wind or spring deities, aren't
            there, on one side? And blossoms and flowers in
            the air. And in the center, Venus, the goddess of
            love. Her golden hair is her only clothing. We
            feast our eyes on that soft, pale flesh. Long legs.
            Long arms. One hand demurely over her breast.
            She's slightly unearthly, and at the same time
            she's the embodiment of feminine beauty and
            physical love. . . . Emmett doesn't reach for his
            sketchbook. He simply stares, agog. And I stare
            with him. Then *at* him. I can see the painting
            reflected in his eyes. He turns and we look at
            each other. The spirit of—

Courtney: After you two leave, I look at the painting. Not
            really at the painting, but at the picture frame.
            It's fancy carved wood. I stare at it hard and for a
            long time. With my Evil Eye.

Elva: Whatever are you talking about?

Courtney: There's no one else there. I stare at one corner
             that's been carved into a flower. And I focus
             my eyes and stare and stare at that flower.
             The varnish on it slowly starts to crack. Then
             it flakes off. I keep on staring. And now
             there's a thin little wisp of smoke coming up
             from it—

Elva: Courtney, stop. Please.

Courtney: And the smoke gets thicker and turns into a little
             flame. That little flame starts moving up the
             frame. And then it spreads onto the canvas. And
             it moves slowly toward Venus's feet. It gets there.
             Her toes blacken and curl up. Then it starts
             climbing those long white legs.

Elva: Stop it this instant! You're ruining the trip.

Courtney: The flame gets bigger. It goes up her legs. It
             divides in two and goes up her arms. Then,
             suddenly, it shoots up her hair. It reaches her
             neck. Then her face. And that entire perfect
             body of hers is twisting and smoking and
             burning! She's completely on fire!

Elva: Courtney, no!

Courtney: Then a flame jumps over to number 3436, *The Adoration of the Magi.*

Elva: Enough! Close the book this instant!

Courtney: And then to number 1316, *The Annunciation.* And then to number 1267, *Magnificat.* And the whole room is catching on fire. We run outside and down the corridor. The fire is racing behind us. It goes through the rooms of Tuscan art. Then the Tribuna. Then the room of various Italian schools. Then the Dutch schools. The Flemish—

Elva: Courtney—I *demand* that you stop!

Courtney: Everyone is running for the stairway. We can feel the heat. We reach the stairs. People are screaming. We run down the 126 steps. We go out the entrance and into the street. We finally stop and look back. The whole Uffizi Gallery is in flames, the whole Italian Renaissance! People are yelling and coughing in the smoke, and the firemen are on their two-hour lunch break and because of that the fire goes wild and the whole building comes crashing—

Elva: *Don't speak another word!* That's my book, not
            yours. I'm coming to get it!

Courtney: And I run through the Piazza, and people
            are chasing me. They know that I did it. But
            I've got the map in my Baedeker. I turn left,
            then right, then down that little alley, then
            across the Arno River on the bridge, then down
            the Via Romana, then left into the Boboli
            Garden—

Elva: Give me that!

Courtney: And I go around the fountain! Then I turn to the
            left! I—

Elva: Courtney, let go!

Courtney: —on that little curvy path! I run—

Elva: *Give it to me!*

Courtney: —in and out through the trees—

Elva: Finally! . . . My Lord! Have you lost your
            mind? . . . Thank heavens the book wasn't
            ripped in half. No more traveling for you!

Certainly not! . . . There was my exercise for the
day. For the week!
[Pause.]
Dear, dear Courtney—I'd have never guessed
this. I can see I'm going to have to hide the
book.

Courtney: No!

Elva: *The trip is over, dear girl.*

Courtney: *[Crying.]* I don't want to come back!

Elva: We'll say we took the train to Genoa, sailed
            to New York, then rode the train to
            Bismarck.

Courtney: No! I'm sorry! I won't do it anymore!

Elva: You've destroyed my trip! Destroyed Italy!

Courtney: I'll stop! I promise!

Elva: You give me no choice.

Courtney: But the trip's all I have! And Edward is there!
            Don't take him away!

Elva: *[Pause.]*
             And who's Edward?

Courtney: A man I met, on the train to Florence.

Elva: You never told me about this.

Courtney: He's a wonderful man. . . . I'll be good! You'll
             see! . . . *Just don't take me to any more places
             like that!*

Elva: *[Long pause.]*
             Dear Courtney. Poor child. *[Sighs.]* I'm
             sorry.
             [Pause.]
             I've been thinking only of Emmett, not of you.
             You who've read so patiently all this time.
             Amidst all my teaching and talking, I'm afraid
             I've been quite insensitive to your feelings. . . . I
             am sorry.
             [Long pause.]
             Maybe the trip doesn't have to end. But I think
             it's best to leave Florence for now. To get away
             from statues and paintings for a while. Perhaps
             we should head into the country.

Courtney: *[Sniffling throughout.]* Could we?

Elva: It's summer. Sweltering. A good time for the
            mountains.

Courtney: Yeah.

Elva: They say the lakes in the north are quite
            beautiful. . . . The flowers at this time of year
            should be lovely. Emmett would appreciate that.

Courtney: He could draw them.

Elva: That's right. And he could practice his landscape
            sketching. . . . I've never been to the Alps.

Courtney: Me neither.

Elva: *[Pause.]*
            Do you think, if I give you back the book, that
            you could find the train schedule?

Courtney: Of course I could.
            [Pause.]
            A morning train or evening train?

Elva: Morning, I think. If that's agreeable to you.

Courtney: That sounds good.

Elva: *[Pause.]*
             Well then. Let's walk back to our hotel. Find the
             map. Make the trip real. Shall we say we're
             walking arm in arm?

Courtney: *[Pause.]*
             I'd like that, Elva.

Ten

Muriel: What did you say your name was again?

Courtney: Courtney.

Muriel: Courtney, of course . . . You're so young to be here.

May: It's snowing snowing snowing again.

Courtney: And that's May.

May: It snows a lot in Italy.

Muriel: I see.

Courtney: You'll get used to her after a while. She thinks she's in Italy.

Muriel: It must be hard for you, living with us old bats.

Courtney: Yeah, well . . . I keep my mind busy.

Muriel: Good for you. I'm the same way. . . . I follow
five different soap operas. And then there's
nighttime TV. Always something to look
forward to.

Courtney: I hate to tell you, but the TV doesn't work.

Muriel: What?

Courtney: Never has worked, since I've been here anyway.
[Pause.]
You like to read?

Muriel: Whole books, you mean?

Courtney: Yeah.

Muriel: I never really had the time. Never got into the
habit. Too busy with farm chores and raising
kids, I guess. Then the grandkids.

Courtney: *[Pause.]*
Got any poems memorized?

Muriel: Poems?

Courtney: Yeah.

Muriel: I don't think so. Not that come to mind . . .
Why do you ask?

Courtney: Because you're gonna need a good imagination
and a good mind to survive in here. Elva
taught me that. She compared a person's
mind to a pantry. Every poem or book
or painting you know is another jar on
the shelf.

Muriel: And who's Elva?

Courtney: She's the one who used to have your bed. She
died last month, after New Year's. Died in
her sleep.

Muriel: Dear me. I'm sorry.

Courtney: That's all right. She lived a long life. And a
happy one. She had lots of love in her life.

Muriel: *[Pause.]*
Are those pictures of your family on your table?

Courtney: Yeah . . . That's a photo of my father.

Muriel: Where was that taken?

Courtney: At the Grand Canyon. A long time ago.

Muriel: He looks like a kind soul.

Courtney: He was.

Muriel: And next to it? The face?

Courtney: That's a drawing he made of my mother. Way
             back when they first met. I still remember those
             earrings from when I was little. My mother's
             favorites. Made out of jade.

Muriel: Really. He drew that?

Courtney: My father was an artist.

May: Elva's not not not with us in Italy
             anymore.

Muriel: What's all this talk about Italy?

Courtney: It's something I'm doing for Edward.

Muriel: And who's that?

Courtney: My boyfriend. I'm taking him on a trip there, in my head, using this old Baedeker guide. It keeps my mind busy. I spend most of the day on that. Right now we've rented a room for two months up north, in the mountains, in Bellagio. On Lake Como.

Muriel: Truly. That's a new one. . . . Saves on airfare, I guess.

Courtney: Do you like the Renaissance?

Muriel: The Renaissance? . . . I really couldn't say.

Courtney: Neither of us are very fond of it. But we love the countryside in Italy. Edward always wanted to go there. But he didn't get the chance. He died last year. From a tumor . . . He asked me if I'd go for him. Then I had my accident. The only way I could go was in my head, but at least I could bring him that way.
[Pause.]
He was blind. He was the nicest person I ever knew. . . . I can't tell you how wonderful it is, being with him. He's not like the boyfriends I had before him. We walk arm in arm, for hours and hours. I can actually feel his arm against

mine. Today we walked all the way to Limonta, along the lake. . . . And when I look up, it's the strangest thing. You won't believe it.

Muriel: What's that?

Courtney: Wherever I am with him, the sky is gold.